LA BELUGA TORTUGA

Hace mucho...ALL DAY!

LA BELUGA TORTUGA

Does A Lot...ALL DAY!

LA BELUGA TORTUGA

Hace mucho...ALL DAY!

A Bilingual English & Spanish Children's Concept Story
By Bobbie Wright Grogan

Bobbie Wright Grogan

LA BELUGA TORTUGA

Does A Lot...ALL DAY!

*A Bilingual English & Spanish Children's Concept Story
By Bobbie Wright Grogan*

Bobbie Wright Grogan

Introduction

This Story's Lovable Main Character, "La Beluga Tortuga" is very different from other Green Sea Turtles; she was born albino white, the color of Beluga Whales. She doesn't let this difference in her outward appearance get in her way to do a lot or "hace mucho" ... ALL DAY!

La Beluga Tortuga teaches children to embrace their own differences and to accept the differences of others in our multicultural and multilingual society. The story line also seeks to inspire and encourage young children to stay active, spend time with family and friends, be thankful, and achieve their goals, no matter what challenges they are dealt in life.

The verbal repetition of the buzz phrase "ALL DAY" within both the Spanish and English texts is present to reiterate the underlying themes of persistence and endurance in pursuit of one's dreams and goals.

Enjoy the Adventure! ¡Vámonos!

La Beluga Tortuga nada y nada;
por el mar azul, ella nada ...

ALL DAY!

La Beluga Tortuga swims and swims;
through the blue sea, she swims ...

ALL DAY!

La Beluga Tortuga juega y juega; con todos sus amigos, ella juega ...

ALL DAY!

La Beluga Tortuga plays and plays;
with all her friends, she plays...

ALL DAY!

La Beluga Tortuga canta y canta;
con su Mamita, ella canta ...

ALL DAY!

La Beluga Tortuga sings and sings;
with her Mommy, she sings ...

ALL DAY!

La Beluga Tortuga se ríe, se ríe; con su Papá, se ríe ...

ALL DAY!

La Beluga Tortuga laughs and laughs; with her Dad, she laughs...

ALL DAY!

La Beluga Tortuga está agradecida; por todas sus bendiciones, está agradecida...

ALL DAY!

La Beluga Tortuga is so thankful; for
all her blessings, she is thankful...

ALL DAY!

El Fin.

¡Gracias por pasar tiempo con nosotros!

The End.

Thanks for spending time with us!

AuthorHouse™
1663 Liberty Drive
Bloomington, IN 47403
www.authorhouse.com
Phone: 1 (800) 839-8640

Published by AuthorHouse 03/27/2019

ISBN: 978-1-7283-0592-9 (sc)
ISBN: 978-1-7283-0591-2 (e)

Library of Congress Control Number: 2019903577

Print information available on the last page.

This book is printed on acid-free paper.

authorHOUSE®

Printed in the United States
By Bookmasters